Rich Penny
Poor Penny

Never Judge a Penny by its Colour

To

You are amazing Keep on being You!

Myia Douglas

Published by

Peaches

Publications

Published in London by Peaches Publications, 2021.

www.peachespublications.co.uk

British Library Cataloguing in Publication Data: A catalogue record for this book is available from the British Library.

ISBN: 9798763408973.

Book cover design: Peaches Publications.

Editor: Winsome Duncan.

Typesetter: Winsome Duncan.

Proof Reader: Linda Green.

Every child should be given the opportunity to share the world through their own eyes. Myia Douglas has demonstrated this in her début publication how she views an element of the world through her eyes.

Claudine Reid MBE

Dedication

I would like to thank Fredrick Douglass, Michael Douglas (daddy), Martina Douglas (mummy) and Aunty Claudine.

Acknowledgements

My Mum and Winsome Duncan from Peaches Publications have assisted me in my book writing journey, by believing in me and encouraging me to bring forth my story.

Preface

I know this is the beginning of my author journey, which I am very grateful to start at seven years old. I have learnt that this process is serious, as you cannot mess around as there are deadlines to meet. Being young I wanted to play and fidget about.

I was dedicated to the project as I went away by myself to write my story on the laptop, which was, me taking responsibility for what I have always wanted to do.

This is my lucky penny
One I'd like to give you
It will not only bring you luck
But help to see you though
Those times when you feel stuck
Or just a little blue.
Whenever you feel you're in a situation,
Where you just can't win
Pull out this Lucky Penny,
And make a simple wish
With this lucky Penny in the palm of your hand,
You will not only have good fortune,
You will have a simple friend

Meet Rich Penny. Many years ago, there was a Rich Penny and a Poor Penny. The Rich Penny was sad and had no friends, yet she lived in a beautiful mansion in the nicest part of town and the Poor Penny lived in high rise estate nearby.

The Pennies lived in the same neighbourhood called Money Ville. So they would see each other around. However Rich Penny was to rich to care or notice anyone else.

One sunny day Poor Penny was walking by Rich Penny's mansion, as he was looking for work. Poor Penny wondered if he would be able to get some work and food for his family there.

Rich Penny was home feeling sick because she was so dirty as she had not been washed or polished in weeks and felt she did not need to regularly as Rich Penny believed she was too rich to have friends.

Poor Penny knocked on Rich Penny's door he said, "may I come in?"

Rich Penny said "yes, yes come in". Only because she was feeling ill. Poor Penny asked, "can I have some work please? so I can buy food for my family, they are very hungry?"

Rich Penny said, " you clean all the leaves out of my seven pools".

Poor Penny thought for a minute well I am extremely hungry, and I need to take care of my family.

"I will do it" said Poor Penny.

That day Poor Penny sweated buckets all afternoon whilst cleaning all seven dirty pools. It was a hot day and the sun shone brightly.

Poor Penny loved his family dearly and wanted to make sure they had food on the table that night.

He was shocked to see Rich Penny's home, which was beautiful however it was so untidy and unkept.

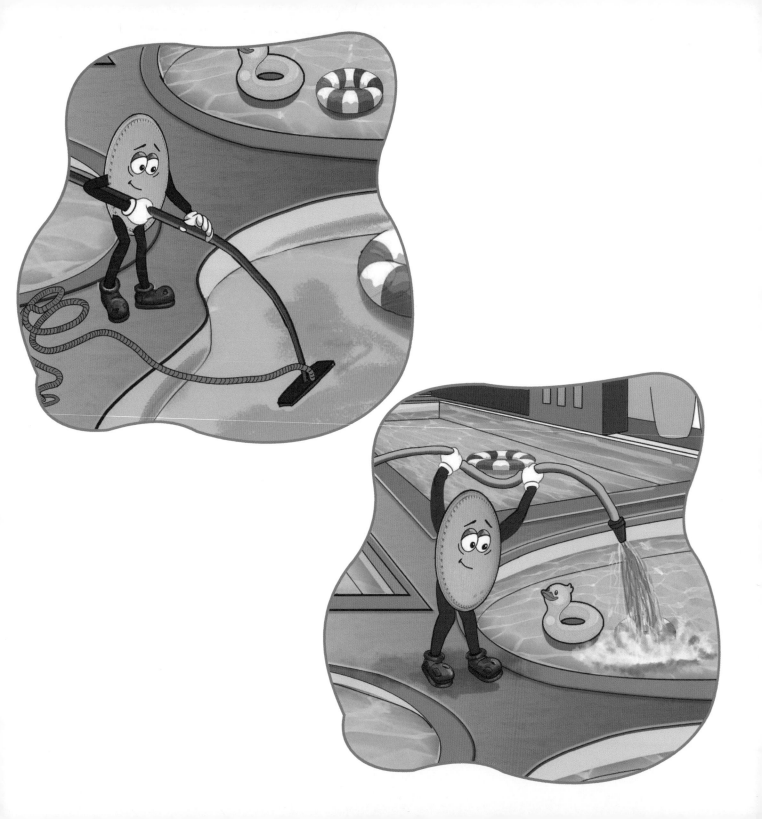

When the job was finally completed Poor Penny said "can I have some food please?". Rich Penny said "yes" Poor Penny took some food, his pay for him and his family and left.

Rich Penny was feeling sad again and very lonely as the only company she had in months left.

A few days later Rich Penny was still feeling unwell, she decided to go on a shopping spree as that always made her feel better.

On this particular day Rich Penny began to notice other Pennies and Notes around her.

On the way home from buying a host of things she did not need or really want, she saw Poor Penny and his family playing in the park which made her feel much better.

Rich Penny told her driver to stop the car and she sat on a bench in the park and watched poor penny and his family having fun.

She wondered how they were so happy without any money.

Rich Penny returned home and looked at all the things in her house along with the things she had bought.

She found it did not make her as happy as watching Poor Penny and his family. That night she went to sleep with lots on her mind...

The next morning Rich Penny woke up determined to be happy. She went to find Poor Penny who lived in the flats.

She said to Poor Penny "I am sorry I made you clean my seven pools when you were hungry. You and your family can come and live with me, I have plenty of space. All I ask is that you share your happiness with me."

The Poor family jumped with joy as their prayers were answered and of course they had lots of happiness to share.

When they arrived at Rich Penny's mansion Poor Penny had a great idea. He spoke to his family and whispered 'In order for Rich Penny to be truly happy she must be washed and polished."

The Poor family all agree to help their new friend Rich Penny to be the happiest version of herself. They brought out the brushes, sponge and with lots of soap and give her a good scrub until she was sparking new.

They all had a big pool party, were they danced, ate and drank late into the night.

Rich Penny was feeling the happiest she has ever been with her new friends.

They laughed and played games and lived happily ever after.

Epilogue

The moral of this story is...never judge.

Self-care, washing, cleaning, and loving you is important.

Friendship and relationships are important to work together as a community, love and family is worth more than money.

About The Author

My Name is Myia Douglas and I am 8 years old. I like to dance, sing and act. I was inspired to write a book by a very famous man from black history called Fredrick Douglass. Which inspired me by thinking just because I am a child it does not mean I cannot write a book or share my gift with the world. You are never too young or too old to shine your light and stay bright.

www.myiadouglas.com

Printed in Great Britain
by Amazon